MIRACLE OF LITTLE TREE

The 9/11 Survivor Tree's Incredible Story

Published in the United States by Inspire Press, LLC

ISBN : 978-1-7352770-1-1

Library of Congress Control Number: 2020912650

Illustrations Copyright Alicia Young Art

First Printing Edition 2020

INSPIRE PRESS,LLC

Port Arthur, TX

From Linda S. Foster and Alicia Young

In memory of all souls lost on September 11, 2001.

In honor of all surviving victims, families, and friends of the September 11th attacks.

With gratitude of all first responders, volunteers, and military personnel who unselfishly

rendered aid; as well as for all workers who diligently and respectfully cleaned the debris,

and then built the National September 11 Memorial & Museum.

With gratefulness for loving and inspiring parents, siblings and spouses:

H. Burton and Vera Foster, Kent Foster ~

Gary and Crystal Templin, David and Jessie Templin, and Blake Young

Dedicated to our own precious miracles who valiantly persevere and inspire each day:

Chris, Zory, and William ~ Leighanne, Adam, Vera, and Stella ~ Andrew ~

and to all future children and grandchildren!

Especially to all young children seeking their own way to be

"brave, strong, and calm" in our ever-challenging world.

"*T*rust in the Lord with all thine heart;

and lean not unto thine own understanding.

In all thy ways acknowledge Him,

and He shall direct thy paths."

Proverbs 3:5-6

In the heart of New York City, near skyscrapers, soaring and shiny,
Grew Little Tree, cute as could be, but who felt ever so small and tiny.
Yet he dearly loved his cozy home, nestled by the mighty Twin Towers.
They made him feel safe, like soldiers guarding him at all hours!

September 11, 2001, sparkled with a sunlit sky on a cloudless day.

Whishing past Little Tree, people were scurrying on their way.

He waved his branches and fluttered his leaves to everyone rushing by.

Friendly Little Tree delighted in all the actions that filled the plaza nearby.

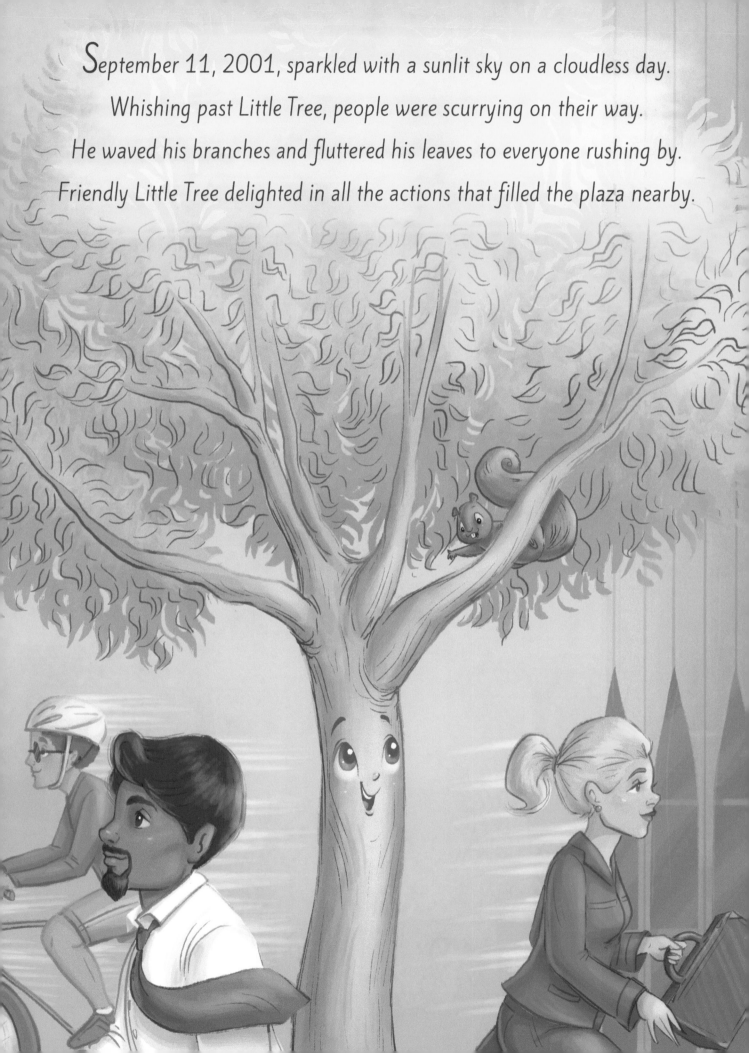

Children laughing, people chatting, tourists gasping, "Ooh!" and "Aah!"

Taxies zooming, bikes zipping; a perfect morning, no doubt at all!

...THEN!

A thunderous rumble – A deafening roar –
An earth-shattering smash and crash!

A startling explosion from up high,
followed by billowing clouds of ash!

SUDDENLY --- UNBELIEVABLY ---
The colossal Twin Towers began to rattle, crumble, and fall!

"Oh, no!" exclaimed Little Tree, realizing the magnitude of it all.

In shock, he didn't even feel the crushing blows from pelting, falling debris,

Breaking his branches, ripping his leaves, and leaving him as a tattered, tiny tree.

Sadly, terrorists had used airplanes to target the Twin Towers nearby.

Destruction was enormous and no one could understand why.

"Be brave, strong, and calm." Little Tree began to think,

"That is what I can do!

Be brave, strong, and calm. That is what I MUST do!"

Swiftly firefighters, police officers, and volunteers, too,

Rushed on the scene to search, recover, and rescue.

Present George W. Bush led as a leader, strong and true.

Little Tree now hoped they'd find him in just a minute or two.

Yet days turned into weeks and no one came his way.

Little Tree was about to give up hope, when in his dismay:

Voices got louder as rescuers came closer,

They started lifting away the debris with mighty bulldozers!

Finally, spying him, one man exclaimed,

"Look here, everybody! It's a live, little tree! ---

In the middle of all this rubble: A MIRACLE! Come see!"

"I don't believe it!" shouted another, "That simply can't be!

Toss it away, nothing's grown here, I can guarantee!"

"Oh no!" panicked Little Tree, "I'm alive! Can't you see?

What will it take for you to truly see me?"

Right at that moment, a swirling wind swept over the scene,

Fluttering Little Tree's last, tiny, remaining leaves of green.

Everyone gasped!

"GREEN LEAVES, GREEN LEAVES!

It's alive, most certainly!"

Cheering and crying, the workers scraped faster to free Little Tree,
For desperately they wanted him to grow and be healthy, you see.
Carefully and gently, they freed him from all the debris,
And readied him for a trip to heal peacefully.

Not knowing where he was going, Little Tree feared it'd be worse.
But once again he calmed himself by remembering his little verse:
"Be brave, strong and calm. That is what I can do!
Be brave, strong and calm. That is what I MUST do!"

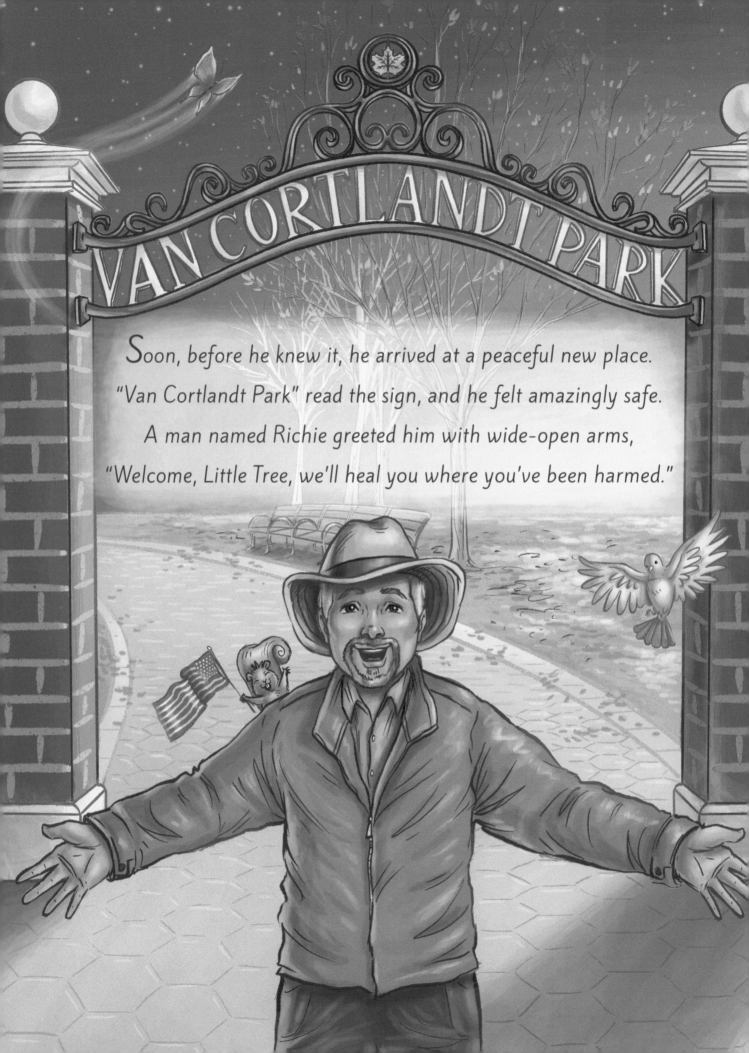

VAN CORTLANDT PARK

Soon, before he knew it, he arrived at a peaceful new place.
"Van Cortlandt Park" read the sign, and he felt amazingly safe.
A man named Richie greeted him with wide-open arms,
"Welcome, Little Tree, we'll heal you where you've been harmed."

Without wasting a minute, Richie's crew got right to work.
Working tirelessly, day and night, their duties no one shirked.

Fertile soil encased his roots like a tender cocoon,
Water softened his jagged branches, bringing forth new blooms.

Warm sunshine comforted him
like a great big, loving hug.
Even a dove made a nest
among his new branches;
safe and snug.

Little Tree cradled it,
just like the Twin Towers
had once guarded him.
While they were now gone,
he cherished their memory
within his every limb.

No longer was he little, for now he was tall.
Even though not as perfect, as when he was small.
They nicknamed him "SURVIVOR TREE" for all that he'd achieved,
Growing, persevering, now thriving; a miracle, indeed!

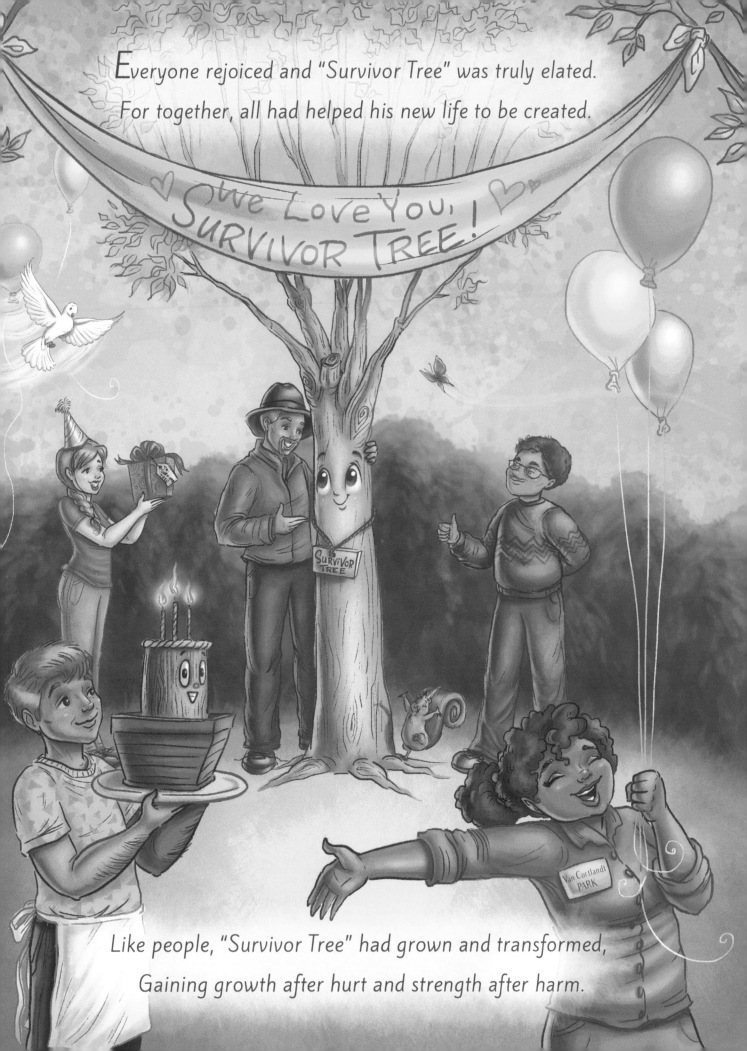

Everyone rejoiced and "Survivor Tree" was truly elated.
For together, all had helped his new life to be created.

WE LOVE YOU, SURVIVOR TREE!

Like people, "Survivor Tree" had grown and transformed,
Gaining growth after hurt and strength after harm.

Then, best of all came, - a surprise and delight:
He was carefully bundled and readied for his home site.

"We're going to miss you, Little Buddy!" Richie said with a tear,

"Yet your story of recovery, the world has to see and hear!"

Waving his branches, he let Richie and his crew know,
"I'll love you forever! My undying love, I'll always show.
I'm certainly not that once perfectly shaped tree,
But I've learned I'm a lot more than just what you see!"

At the 9/11 Memorial, he was planted like a precious jewel,
By the Memorial Glade and symbolic, twin reflection pools.
While his deep ridges and scars show his hurt from the past,
They also display his great efforts to survive and to last.

People from the world over, now flock by his side :

A symbol of heroic efforts, all can find deep inside.

Then as people step closer, they see new limbs too.

Surprisingly, they are not rough, but sleek and ever so smooth!

A reminder that everyone can create fresh, new starts,
With inner strength and help from loving hearts,
Remembering to never give up, or wither from within,
For the hurt is the point from where the real healing begins!

Each spring, as "Survivor Tree's" blossoms come into sight,
They burst open into brilliant clusters of white!
People look up, and in their hearts say a prayer
For the ones lost, the ones saved, and loved ones everywhere.

Definitely, there's mighty power from deep within us all!

No matter what we look like; whether our problems are big or small.

We have strength to face our challenges, from sunup to nightfall.

If we keep trying, we can certainly conquer them one and all.

And when we see others who need a helping hand,

Quick as a wink, we can jump into action, for we understand:

TOGETHER we're stronger and mightier than ever,

By helping each other, we can change the world forever!

With faith, hope, and prayer,
Just like Little Tree, we each can declare:
"Be brave, strong, and calm. That is what I can do!
Be brave, strong, and calm. That is what I MUST do!"

THE
END